Fame School

Lucky Break

Cindy Jefferies

USBORNE

For Chris – my one and only big brother.

First published in 2005 by Usborne Publishing Ltd., Usborne House,
83-85 Saffron Hill, London EC1N 8RT, England. www.usborne.com

Copyright © 2005 by Cindy Jefferies. The right of Cindy Jefferies to be identified
as the author of this work has been asserted by her in accordance with the
Copyright, Designs and Patents Act, 1988.

The name Usborne and the devices ♀ ⊕ are Trade Marks of
Usborne Publishing Ltd.

This is a work of fiction. The characters, incidents, and dialogues are products of the
author's imagination and are not to be construed as real. Any resemblance to actual events
or persons, living or dead, is entirely coincidental.

A CIP catalogue record for this book is available from the British Library.

JFMAMJJASO D/05

ISBN 0 7460 6836 0

Printed in Great Britain.

Ta

room!

me and fortur

d be one step a   y!

Welcome to

Fame School

For another fix of

read

Reach for the Stars

Rising Star

Secret Ambition

Rivals!

Tara's Triumph

1 Marmalade

"Two more Rising Stars points! *Two!*" Marmaduke Stamp, always known as Marmalade, waggled his wildly corkscrewed ginger hair in triumph. His friend, Danny James, smiled, glanced at his own grade card and put it quietly in his bag.

The two friends couldn't have been less alike. Marmalade's long curls, snub nose and freckled face were as noticeable as his bubbly nature and noisy laugh. Everything about him was larger than life, especially when he'd just got a bit closer to his ambition. He was desperate to dance at the Rising Stars Concert, which was recorded at the local television studios in front of an invited audience of important people from the entertainment industry. *Everyone* wanted to get on the show, but only the very best would be chosen. Marmalade so hoped that the concert would be his big break.

Performances at their last school concert, an amazing outdoor charity affair organized by Tara Fitzgerald, had counted towards Rising Stars points, and Marmalade had been waiting anxiously all over half term to find out how he'd done. Now he knew, and was sure his excitement would make him unstoppable. During the holiday, he had spent time teaching himself some hip-hop moves and now he wanted to demonstrate them to Danny.

"Watch this!" he said, flipping neatly into a handstand.

"Wow!" Danny smiled. But Marmalade hadn't finished. He walked a couple of metres on his hands and then, in one fluid movement, rolled over and jumped back onto his feet. Danny was seriously impressed.

Marmalade grinned. "Street dancing is the way to go!" he announced. "There are so many cool moves."

And with that, he crouched down in the corridor and started to spin on his shoulders. After a couple of spins, he collapsed in a sprawl of arms and legs, getting in the way of several other students.

Danny laughed. "Maybe you should save it for outside," he said.

"For goodness' sake!" protested Tara, who had to step over him to get past. "What are you doing?"

Marmalade grinned. He loved to tease Tara, who was often grumpy. "Polishing the floor," he told her, getting to his feet. "Does it look better now? Actually," he added to Danny as Tara scowled at him and marched off, "the reason I couldn't spin properly was that the floor wasn't shiny enough. Too much friction, you see. Some street dancers even carry a big piece of cardboard around wherever they go to give themselves a good surface."

"It sounds a bit of a pain to have to do that," said Danny.

"That's not the right attitude for a street dancer!" Marmalade insisted, spinning round on one leg, in a movement more like ballet than anything else.

"Just as well I'm not a dancer, then," Danny reminded him with a smile.

Danny was a drummer, and both he and Marmalade were at Rockley Park, the school of their dreams. It was a brilliant boarding school that taught students everything they needed to know about making it in the music business, as well as providing all the usual school lessons.

Marmalade had won a place at Rockley Park for his talented and exuberant dancing. He had a good singing voice too, but dance was his life, and his ambition was to star in all the best pop videos.

"Come on!" he urged Danny. "Let's see what grades the others have got!" He flung his bag over his shoulder and raced off in the direction of the dining hall, leaving Danny to follow on behind.

Marmalade soon caught up with twins Pop and Lolly Lowther – famous for their modelling success – and flung himself between them, draping his arms round their shoulders.

"Marmalade! Get off!" Pop laughed, wriggling free and smoothing her long, black hair back into place.

Lolly disentangled herself too. "What's up?" she asked.

"Grades!" Marmalade said, beaming all over his face. "And I've done it again. I've got two more Rising Stars points. That *must* make me good enough to dance at the Rising Stars Concert." He grabbed Lolly again and whirled her round.

"Maybe," conceded Pop, avoiding Marmalade and her sister, who were still spinning. "But don't forget that the final decision isn't made until nearly the end of term. You can't relax yet."

"I know," Marmalade agreed. He stopped whirling Lolly, let her go and looked serious for a moment. "But they always want a good mix of students, and there aren't *that* many people who are specializing in dance. I *have* to have a good chance."

"I'm sure you do," Lolly agreed, still catching her breath. "You're by far the best dancer in our year. And I know how much you want this chance."

Lucky Break

"We *all* do!" her sister protested. "The Rising Stars Concert could be brilliant for *our* careers too, Lolly. Think of the audience." She shivered with anticipation. "There'll be loads of important people there from the music industry, all ready to sign up the best acts! And that's before the programme even goes on air!"

"But you're already famous models," Marmalade protested. "And you're halfway to being famous pop stars as well. For me, appearing at a Rising Stars Concert could give me the lucky break I'm looking for."

Danny caught them up, and Lolly turned to him as they all reached the dining room.

"How did you get on with *your* grades, Danny?" she asked. "Did you get any Rising Stars points?"

He nodded seriously. "Yes," he said. "But my maths grade was down."

"Never mind that!" Marmalade told him. "Own up. How many Rising Stars points did you get? I forgot to ask earlier. I was so excited about my two."

Danny looked embarrassed. "I got three," he admitted.

"Three!" squealed Pop. "*Nobody* gets three. I thought two was the most you could get for each subject."

Marmalade's mouth dropped open, and he stared at Danny in amazement, but his generous nature didn't allow him to be jealous for more than a second or two.

"Well!" he laughed, clapping Danny on the back. "Thank goodness you're not a dancer, or I'd have no chance! Well done! Come on, let's get some food. I'm starving." He spun round on one leg and headed in through the door towards the lunch queue.

Most of the students were comparing their grades over lunch. And it wasn't all good news. Rockley Park didn't allow its students to shirk their academic work, however musically talented they were. Anyone who dropped grades knew that they would have to study hard during the second half of term to make up lost ground.

Although Lolly had improved most of *her* grades, the coolest singer in the class, Chloe Tompkins, needed to work harder at maths like Danny, and Tara, who played bass guitar, had dropped grades in geography and physics.

Marmalade was down in most of his academic grades, but nothing could dampen his high spirits. "I'm on my way to the Rising Stars Concert!" he sang as they headed off for their next lesson, flinging his arms wide and almost hitting Tara in the process.

Tara ducked just in time and glowered at Marmalade. "Pride comes before a fall," she warned him crossly.

But Marmalade wasn't going to let Tara spoil his mood. "You only fall if you're not properly balanced," he told her pompously, pirouetting in a rather more controlled manner. "And as a dancer I am *always* well balanced," he added.

Tara snorted in derision. "Your body might be balanced," she said. "But I'm not so sure about your brain. Can't you see that you're in the way?" She pushed past him and stalked down the corridor ahead of everyone else.

"Tara! Don't leave us!" he called after her in mock despair. "We need you!"

Chloe giggled. "Don't tease her, Marmalade," she protested. "You know she doesn't like it."

In geography, Marmalade was in too much of a silly mood to work properly. Apart from dance lessons, he found most of the work difficult, even when he was trying hard, and when he got excited about his dancing he found it impossible to concentrate. His geography teacher wasn't impressed by his behaviour, and he was told off in English as well. Everyone was supposed to be writing poetry about their favourite things, but Marmalade's silly efforts had almost the whole class giggling.

"*Dance is lovely,*" he read out when it was his turn. "*Dance is fun. Especially when Tara does it and falls on her bum.*"

But Tara wasn't laughing, and neither was their teacher. "That isn't poetry," Mrs. Hale told Marmalade. "It's just a silly rhyme, and it doesn't even scan properly. You're not trying."

"I *am*," he protested, rolling his eyes wildly and making the class laugh even harder.

Lucky Break

His teacher wasn't impressed. "I want six *sensible* lines about dance by tomorrow afternoon, or you'll end up in more trouble," she told him. "You're not usually *this* silly, Marmalade. What's got into you today?"

"Rising Stars points," he told her. "I got two more this time. I'm ahead of the other dancers in my group and I just *know* I'm going to dance at the Rising Stars Concert at the end of term."

"Well, that's very good news for you," the teacher agreed. "And I'm not surprised you're excited. But *do* try not to disrupt lessons. It's not fair on the other students, however much they enjoy your clowning. And with your grades, you can't afford to waste lesson time either."

"That was lucky," Danny told him after the lesson. "I thought you were really going to get into trouble."

Marmalade smiled at his friend. "I'm an *artist*!" he said, launching himself into a tremendous jump and turning in mid-air. He landed neatly beside Danny with a huge grin on his face. "English and geography grades won't make a bit of difference when I'm making pop videos," he said. "I don't care how much the teachers grumble. *Nothing* is going to stop me now. No matter what happens, I'm going to be dancing in the Rising Stars Concert. I just know it!"

2 Long-suffering Teachers

In biology, they were studying how an eye worked and Mrs. Pinto, the science teacher, wanted to show the class some slides. "Marmalade, will you pull the blinds down, please?" she asked.

He leaped up, knocking over his stool with a clatter and sliding into the workbench in front of the window.

Some people started giggling, but Mrs. Pinto looked cross. "You can't afford to fool about in my lessons," she told him, "or you'll get an even worse grade next time. Now pick up that stool and sit down."

It was no use. When Marmalade was in this sort of mood, he found it impossible to behave. Everything seemed funny to him.

His whispered comments during the slide show were too quiet for Mrs. Pinto to hear, but they made it difficult for his friends not to laugh out loud. Lolly, who loved biology, and was trying hard to concentrate, got very frustrated.

"Be quiet," she hissed. She leaned over and poked Marmalade in the back, but if she'd hoped this would make him behave, she was sadly mistaken. Instead, he wildly overreacted.

"Ooh!" he yelped, jerking upright and looking so affronted that the people closest to him burst out laughing.

By now, Mrs. Pinto was really angry and sent him outside for the rest of the lesson. "If you can't behave, you're not welcome in my class," she told Marmalade. "You can sit outside until we're finished, and you'll have to copy up the work later."

"I don't care," Marmalade told Danny afterwards. "Mrs. Pinto has no feelings!" His imitation of Mrs. Pinto telling him off had Danny in fits of laughter.

The next lesson was general dance. For the first

couple of years at Rockley Park, all the students were required to study dance as part of their education. It was an excellent way to keep fit, and helped to develop poise and balance. For the dedicated dance students, there were extra lessons as a special group, when they studied modern dance, jazz and Marmalade's favourite, freestyle, which suited his imagination and energy so well. But today, the lesson was for the whole class, and less demanding of Marmalade's talents. He always enjoyed dancing, so he was happy to cruise along in this lesson, but his favourite time of all was when the dance teacher, Mr. Penardos, gave him some one-to-one tuition in the special dance group. That was when he worked his hardest and learned the most.

Everyone was full of energy after the half-term break, so when they had completed their warming-up stretches, Mr. Penardos put on some bouncy music and got everyone to jog on the spot for a few minutes.

"Keep it going!" he urged. "Follow me. Arms up

two...three...and down two...three... Step forward, ver' nice Pop, and back two...three..."

As they worked their way through a simple routine, Marmalade didn't bother to concentrate much. He could do the movements almost without thinking. While they were having a brief rest, he nudged the boy next to him, Martin, who was another talented dancer.

"I bet I can imitate people while I'm dancing," Marmalade said. "I've been watching them. Everyone does the movements slightly differently."

"Go on, then," Martin urged him. "Do Tara. She should be easy enough."

Marmalade stood up and glared out into space. Then he began to jog stiffly. He looked exactly like Tara when she was concentrating hard doing something that she didn't really like.

Martin laughed. "Do some more people," he said, but Marmalade had to stop because Mr. Penardos was ready for the next routine.

As the lesson went on, there was more and more giggling from Marmalade's end of the room. He was entertaining his friends by imitating them and he had copied them all perfectly. There was Chloe, with her energetic and enthusiastic movements, which sometimes went very wrong. There was Ed Henderson, a guitarist putting up with dance because he had to, but obviously not enjoying it one bit, and serious and professional Pop and Lolly.

"Thank you, Marmalade," said Mr. Penardos. "That's very clever, but you are disrupting my class.

"Okay, everyone." Mr. Penardos stopped the music and spoke to the whole class. "Now don' forget to warm down those muscles. This is as important as the warm-up at the beginning of class. We don't want any injuries, do we? Marmalade, can you stay behind for a moment, please?"

"Now you're for it!" warned Martin. "Hard luck!"

But Mr. Penardos didn't want to tell Marmalade off. "I realize you're bored in this class," he told Marmalade when the others had gone. "But you should treat it as an opportunity to keep your fitness up. Don' make the mistake of thinking you're too good to do simple exercises. They keep you supple and help you to avoid injury."

Marmalade nodded, but Mr. Penardos hadn't finished. "A new dancer is joining us tomorrow," he added. "We wouldn't usually start someone so near the end of the school year, but his parents have recently moved to this country from Hong Kong, and they were anxious to get him into school right away. We auditioned him over half term, and were very impressed. He has a strong classical background to his dancing, which you migh' find interesting."

Marmalade kept his expression neutral. He wasn't sure he liked the idea of a new student arriving who might be better than him.

"Don't worry!" Mr. Penardos said with a laugh, as if he'd read Marmalade's mind. "He won't steal your glory. You can teach him plenty abou' freestyle dancing. He needs to learn all abou' modern styles, but he'll make an excellent addition to our class, so I hope you'll make an effort to get on with him."

"Okay," said Marmalade, sounding a bit more

enthusiastic. Rockley Park taught some classical ballet, but the emphasis was very much on modern dance. It sounded to Marmalade as if he would still be top dog, and he might be able to pick up some tips from the new boy as well.

"He's not confident like you," Mr. Penardos went on. "He's quite shy, and is sure to need some help settling in, so I wondered if you'd like to look after him for a bit?"

Marmalade's eyes lit up. That sounded fun! He would enjoy being in charge and showing the new boy around. "Of course I will," he agreed, his mind running ahead. He would soon put a new student at ease and share all his knowledge about the most laid-back teachers – and those he would have to watch out for. And a new student would be a new audience for all his jokes and antics! "What's his name?" Marmalade asked Mr. Penardos.

"Jack Cheung," said his teacher. "He is a very talented dancer with real promise. But it's not going to be easy for him, joining us almos' at the end of the school year, and having jus' come from abroad. Everything will be new for him. Will you take him under your wing...without leading him astray?" he added.

Marmalade grinned. "Yeah!" he agreed. "It'll be great to have another real dancer. We're such a small group."

"Good." Mr. Penardos smiled. "Maybe having a bit of responsibility for someone else will help you settle down a bit. I know some of the other teachers think you can be a bit too exuberant."

After showering, Marmalade went to his room. Danny was there already and so were his other two roommates, guitarists Ben and Ed.

"Did Mr. Penardos tell you off for fooling about?" asked Danny.

Marmalade grinned. "No, I got away with it," he told him. "And he gave me some interesting news."

"What's that?" asked Ben.

"A new student is coming," Marmalade announced. "Another dancer. Mr. Penardos has asked me to look after him until he gets settled in."

"He's missed almost the whole year!" Ed exclaimed. "It seems a weird time to change schools."

"He's just come from Hong Kong," Marmalade told his friends. "His parents want him to get settled as soon as possible."

"If it were me," said Ed, "I'd have tried to wangle a few weeks' extra holiday and start school next term!"

"Maybe he did try, but his parents wouldn't let him," said Marmalade, wanting to stick up for his new charge.

"I wonder which bedroom Mr. South will put him in?" said Ben. "Ravi has a spare bed in his room, and so does Charlie, now Robbie's left."

"Ravi's room, I hope," Danny said. "Charlie might be a bit of a pain to a new kid."

"Don't worry," Marmalade said. "Wherever he is, he'll be fine with *me* looking after him!"

3 New Boy

The next morning, Mr. South called Ravi and Marmalade into his study after breakfast.

"This is Jack Cheung," the housemaster said, introducing a slightly built boy who looked very nervous. "I'm putting Jack in your room, Ravi. So, could you show him around the house and help him settle in?" Then he turned to Marmalade. "Mr. Penardos has told me that you'll take care of Jack during the school day," he added.

"Yeah," said Marmalade. "No problem."

"Good," said Mr. South. "It's tough joining a school halfway through a term, but I know you'll all make Jack welcome and help him out."

Lucky Break

The boys had to hurry to assembly, and then afterwards there was no time for Jack to meet Marmalade's friends as they headed to their first class.

"I'll introduce you to everyone later," Marmalade told Jack, feeling very important. "Come on, we'd better get going. We don't want to be late for dance."

It didn't take long to get changed into the loose trousers and T-shirts needed for the lesson. Mr. Penardos was waiting for them in the studio. The class was small. Only five students in Marmalade's year were taking dance as their major subject, but every one of them was utterly dedicated.

"Welcome to our group, Jack," Mr. Penardos said. "Meet Martin, Ellie, Megan and Alice. I expect Marmalade and Martin will be glad to have another boy!"

Jack smiled shyly. Marmalade showed him where to leave his towel before taking him over to the full-length mirror at the far end of the room.

"I suppose you're used to warming up before lessons, aren't you?" Marmalade asked, as everyone began their stretching exercises.

Jack watched as Marmalade carefully lifted one arm above his head and used his other hand to push the arm back over his shoulder. "Yes," he agreed. "I know similar exercises, but these aren't exactly the same as the ones I use. Do you mind if I copy you? I expect I'll soon get them right."

Marmalade grinned. "That's fine," he said. "And if you're not sure about anything, just ask."

"I have a question," said Jack right away.

"Go on, then," said Marmalade, ready to explain the finer points of the stretch he was doing.

"I hope you don't mind," Jack said, then hesitated. "Why are you called Marmalade?"

Marmalade burst out laughing. "It's because of my hair," he explained, tossing back his long, curly ginger hair. My real name is Marmaduke, but it's such a terrible name that even the teachers call me Marmalade."

"I see," said Jack, smiling. "It's a cool name."

"Thanks!" said Marmalade, liking Jack more every minute.

Jack kept watching Marmalade, and had soon

learned Mr. Penardos's favourite warm-up routine. Once they had stretched their muscles, they were ready to move on to the lesson. Although they were all concentrating hard on Mr. Penardos's instructions, Jack kept looking at Marmalade to reassure himself that he was following properly. He seemed very grateful to have Marmalade nearby, and even though Jack was a talented ballet dancer, his lack of knowledge as far as modern dance was concerned made Marmalade feel rather superior.

"This half term, I want you all to create your own individual dances," Mr. Penardos announced at the end of the lesson. "You've learned a lot over the past year. Let's see if you can put it into practice." Mr. Penardos looked at Marmalade. "Perhaps you can help Jack a little," he suggested. "I know you have only just joined us," he added to Jack, "but have a go anyway. Don' look so worried! It's not an exam!"

While Jack was fetching his towel, Mr. Penardos had a quiet word with Marmalade. "I expect he'll need you less as he gets used to the way we do things here," he told him.

"Oh, I don't mind," said Marmalade enthusiastically. "It's like having a little brother, instead of all the sisters I'm lumbered with at home!"

"That's all right, then!" laughed Mr. Penardos.

At lunchtime, Marmalade took Jack over to the dining hall. "The salads are good," he advised the new boy, "but don't bother with the pasta."

Jack glanced at the hot dish of the day, but took Marmalade's advice and chose a cheese salad instead. At Marmalade's friends' table, everyone moved up a bit so Jack could join them. The morning had been so busy that he hadn't had an opportunity to meet them properly yet.

"Chloe, Tara, Pop and Lolly," said Marmalade, waving his arm towards the girls. "And these are my roommates, Ed, Ben and Danny."

"Did you enjoy your first dance class?" asked Lolly. "Pop and I love dancing, but our major subject is singing."

"It was great!" Jack said shyly. "Mr. Penardos is a good teacher, but I have so much to learn quickly. I am lucky to have Marmalade to help me. He is an excellent teacher too."

"Wow!" said Pop grinning at him. "Don't swell Marmalade's head any more, will you? He's bad enough already!"

Jack blushed. But Marmalade was pleased at Jack's praise and grinned. "Well," he told Pop carelessly, "I just happen to explain things brilliantly!"

"Hmm!" grunted Tara. "Like you explained map references to me when I'd missed a bit of geography because of my bass lesson overrunning?"

Marmalade had forgotten that. "I just got a bit muddled!" he protested.

"You certainly did!" laughed Chloe. "You explained the references the wrong way round, so poor Tara couldn't find anything she was supposed to on the map!"

"All right!" Marmalade agreed hurriedly, not wanting Jack to hear anything bad about him. "I suppose you never muddle anything, like giving your hairdresser the wrong instructions?"

There was silence for a moment. Everyone had been avoiding the subject of Chloe's hair. She had had it cut over half term, and it was obvious that she really hated the ultra-short cut. She'd taken to wearing a black beanie over it, which didn't suit her very well either.

Chloe's mouth opened and then closed again. Tears welled up in her eyes.

Marmalade wanted to say sorry, but he wanted to impress Jack even more. "Don't worry, it'll soon grow!" he told her breezily and picked up his tray. "Come on," he added to Jack. "I'll introduce you to some more people."

Jack half smiled at the others and followed Marmalade to another table.

"Charlie!" Marmalade said. "Can we join you? This is Jack."

"I'm just going," Charlie Owen told them. "Hi-Jack!" he added, laughing uproariously at his own feeble joke.

"Take no notice," Marmalade said as the other boy left. "Charlie likes to think he's tough, but he shouldn't give you any trouble. If he does, make sure you tell me straight away and I'll sort him out."

"Thanks, Marmalade," said Jack gratefully. He glanced back at Marmalade's friends. "Are they all cross with you about what you said to Chloe?" he added.

Marmalade followed his gaze uncomfortably. He wished he hadn't teased Chloe. She obviously felt terrible about her new haircut, but Marmalade had long ago come to terms with his own outrageous hair, and things like that didn't trouble him any more. Surely Chloe ought to be able to cope with a bit of teasing?

"They'll come round," he said hopefully. "Chloe's usually quite good at taking a joke. Maybe she's had a bad day..."

"There weren't any girls at my last school," Jack told him. "And I don't have any sisters. I suppose being at a mixed school has helped you understand girls."

"Er...I suppose so," said Marmalade, not so sure he'd handled the situation very well at all. But, if Jack thought he'd done well, maybe he had? Yes, perhaps

Chloe was just being silly. Apologizing wouldn't have helped. Far better to jolly her out of it, or make a joke of it.

Marmalade looked over at the table again and caught Pop's eye. He winked and tossed his bright ginger curls towards her. He made cutting motions with his hand, as if he was chopping his own hair off. Pop nudged Tara and they both watched as Marmalade mimed horror at his supposedly newly bald head. But the girls didn't laugh. Instead, they looked angry and turned away. Marmalade sighed. It might be better to give the girls a wide berth for a while. But it didn't matter because he had Jack to look after. That was much more important right now.

4 Friends

Jack was keeping Marmalade very busy with all the questions he had about Rockley Park.

"Who's your favourite teacher? Do you get into big trouble if homework isn't in on time? Do you ever get to perform outside school?"

Marmalade was more than happy to tell him about the Rising Stars Concert at the end of the school year. "It's only a half-hour programme," he explained. "So just the very best students in the school can perform. That usually means the senior students, of course, but everyone has a chance. The teachers award points throughout the year, and at school concerts students can vote for who they like too. The final decision on who can perform is taken near the end of this term, which is why I'm so excited to have so many points for my dancing. It would be so amazing to dance on TV!"

Every day Jack listened intently to everything Marmalade told him and worked hard to fit in. He was still quite shy though. "It's great having you for a friend," he told Marmalade. "I didn't really have any friends at my last school."

"Why not?" asked Marmalade.

"It was just an ordinary school," Jack confessed. "And once some kids discovered I went to ballet lessons after school, they teased me so much that they made my life a misery. No one would be friends with me after that."

"That's terrible," Marmalade said. "But why did you come to Rockley Park, if ballet is your favourite subject? You should have gone to a special ballet school. We don't do much ballet here, except for the basics."

"I think it will be useful to be trained in modern dance," said Jack. "So few people make it to the top in classical ballet, but there are lots more opportunities in the sort of dancing you do. My parents were keen for me to keep up my ballet, but I think this will be better. That's why I auditioned to come here."

"Well, you don't need to worry about anyone teasing you about your dancing at *this* school," Marmalade told him.

Jack didn't seem quite so sure. "You won't tell everyone I used to study ballet, will you?" he begged Marmalade. "I shouldn't have told you really, I suppose."

"Well, all right," agreed Marmalade. "I won't say anything if you don't want me to."

Jack continued to stick to Marmalade like a limpet and Marmalade loved having someone looking up to him.

The rest of Marmalade's gang would have been happy to hang out with Jack too, but Marmalade and Jack were spending so much time together that there wasn't really any chance for Jack to make any other friends. And Marmalade found himself spending less time with his old friends as well. When they met Danny, Ed and Ben one afternoon after lessons, Marmalade realized that he'd hardly spoken to them in the past few days.

"Hi!" he said as they approached. "What are you lot up to?"

"We're going to jam over at the Rock Department," Danny told him. "Come with us. You can be our vocalist, if you like."

"Sounds fun," agreed Marmalade. "Are you going to come, Jack?"

Jack hesitated. "I don't think so," he said. "Thanks, but I don't sing or play anything. I think I'll go and practise those dance steps Mr. Penardos said I ought to concentrate on."

Marmalade clapped his hands to his head. "Oh, yes!" he agreed. "I'd forgotten. I promised to run through the routine with you. Sorry."

"It's all right," said Jack. "You can show me later."

Marmalade shook his head. "No way," he said. "I know Mr. Penardos wanted you to learn them quickly so you can progress to the next group of steps. It's better if I run through them first – otherwise your practice time could be wasted. I'll come with you now."

"What about your jam session?" asked Jack.

"It's all right," said Danny. "Ed can sing. He's not *that* bad!"

Ed laughed. "Thanks!" he said. "I'll have you know that some people really rate my voice!"

"Sorry, mate," Marmalade told Danny. "Next time, maybe."

"Sorry about that," said Jack, once Danny and the others had gone.

"Don't worry," Marmalade told him, moonwalking down the corridor. "Danny and the others are always jamming. I can join in with them any time. And I'd rather be dancing than singing any day!"

When they got to the practice room, Marmalade showed Jack the routine and Jack copied him. It wasn't long before Jack knew every step and Marmalade watched as he went through the routine once more on his own.

"That's great!" said Marmalade. He was very impressed by Jack's fluid and graceful movements. His classical training shone through with every step he took. Marmalade realized that he could learn some really useful things from his new friend.

"Can you can tell me what this is called in ballet terms?" asked Marmalade. He took a huge breath and leaped high, turning in the air and landing with a thump of trainers on the wooden floor.

Jack frowned. "Well," he mused, "if you'd had one foot pulled up to the knee of your other leg while you'd been doing it, I think it would be called a *saut de basque,* but I've never done one. Ballet dancers usually land more gently too."

Marmalade grinned. "I like dancing noisily," he said. "That's why I'm glad we only need the basics of ballet here. Have you seen the group of professional dancers who dance in their wellies? And there's another lot who bang sticks, dustbin lids and all sorts of stuff to keep rhythm. They make plenty of noise!"

Much later, when everyone was getting ready for bed

and Jack was in the bedroom he shared with Ravi and two others, Marmalade listened to his friends talking about the jam session that he hadn't joined in with. He felt a twinge of disappointment that he'd missed out because of Jack. Jam sessions with his old friends were always fun, and he didn't seem to have done anything but dancing since Jack joined the school.

"Sorry I couldn't join you," he said.

"That's all right," Danny told him. "Don't worry, it wasn't important."

"You have rather taken over Jack, haven't you?" Ben said, climbing into bed and grabbing a book.

"Well, he is new," said Marmalade. "And Mr. Penardos did ask me to take care of him."

"He's been here for a while now, though," Ed pointed out. "Shouldn't he be standing on his own two feet a bit more?"

Marmalade shrugged. "He told me he's not very good at making friends. He's very shy."

"Well, don't forget the rest of us while you're monopolizing Jack," Ed warned him.

Marmalade flushed. "I'm not monopolizing him!" he said crossly. "He can talk to anyone he likes!"

"Chloe's still a bit upset about what you said to her," Danny told him quietly. "I know you didn't mean to be unkind, but she's really down about her hair. She told me yesterday that it seems to be taking for ever to grow."

"The girls do seem to be a bit against me just now," Marmalade admitted.

"They're just rallying round Chloe," Danny explained. "Why don't you talk to her? I'm sure you could make her feel better if you tried."

"Okay," agreed Marmalade. "I shouldn't have teased her, should I? But I didn't realize she'd be quite so upset. I'll speak to her tomorrow."

In the morning, Marmalade decided not to wait for Jack before he went to breakfast. He wanted to make up with Chloe, but he didn't really want Jack to witness his apology.

Luckily for Marmalade, most of the girls were early risers, and Chloe was already having her breakfast with Tara, Pop and Lolly when he reached the dining room.

Lucky Break

"Hi there!" said Marmalade, sliding into the empty seat opposite Chloe. Her beanie was pulled down well over her ears, and Marmalade felt sorry that he'd been so insensitive about her hair.

Chloe gave Marmalade a slight smile before turning away, but Pop was more vocal. "Hi, Danny!" she said cheerfully, as he joined them. She ignored Marmalade completely. She wasn't going to make it easy for him.

Marmalade leaned over and gently nudged Chloe's arm. She looked at him reluctantly. "What do you want?" she asked.

"I'm sorry about the other day," he told her. "I didn't mean to upset you. I should have remembered how I used to hate my hair."

"Did you?" Chloe asked, looking at his wild, bright ginger hair. "I can't imagine that. It's so much a part of you."

"Well, it was either get used to the way it is or be miserable," he admitted. "And I decided a couple of years ago that I didn't want to be miserable, so I let it grow and become even wilder. I really like it now."

"I *hate* mine at the moment," Chloe told him, tugging the beanie even lower. "I told the hairdresser I wanted it short, but I'm practically *bald*." She lowered her voice. "And now my ears stick out. It's horrible."

"Well, your hair *will* grow," Marmalade assured her sympathetically. "And hats are quite cool at the moment. I'm really sorry I teased you. Friends?"

Chloe nodded. "Friends," she agreed.

"Thank goodness!" Marmalade put his hand on his heart and rolled his eyes.

Chloe laughed. "I'm glad we're friends again," she said. "It hasn't been the same without you clowning around at mealtimes."

"Yes," agreed Lolly. "We've missed you, Marmalade."

Marmalade grinned. It seemed that now Chloe had forgiven him, the rest of the girls were willing to be friends again too. "Well, I've been busy," he told them. "But I'm here now, and I can tell you that I've been learning some cool new jumps. I can even do a *saut de basque*!"

"Whatever's that?" asked Pop.

"It's French for a really tricky jump," Marmalade told her airily. "Even some quite good ballet dancers can't do a *saut de basque*!"

"Whoever has been teaching you ballet steps?" giggled Chloe.

It was on the tip of Marmalade's tongue to tell them about Jack being a ballet dancer, but then he caught sight of him coming into the dining room and remembered that Jack hadn't wanted anyone to know about that.

"I just did it instinctively!" he said grandly. "And then I looked up the name in the library."

"You fibber," laughed Pop. "Someone must have been teaching you some ballet terms. I can't believe you've been reading about them!"

"Got to go," Marmalade told the girls. Jack was coming over and Marmalade didn't want them guessing that he was the ballet expert. "Come on, Jack," he said rather pompously, not giving him a chance to put his tray on the table. "Let's go and sit over there with the other dancers."

As they moved away, the girls burst out laughing. Jack looked at Marmalade with a worried face. "What were they laughing at?" he asked.

"Don't worry, not you," Marmalade reassured him. "Or me," he added uncertainly. "Probably just some silly girl stuff."

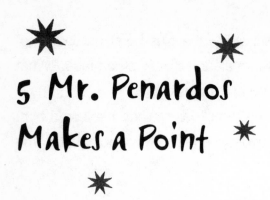

5 Mr. Penardos Makes a Point

At the next general dance class, Mr. Penardos had a surprise for everyone.

"Some of you will need to sing and dance at the same time when you perform," he told them. "And you will have to get used to wearing a special microphone like this." He held up a small headset, and Marmalade exchanged excited glances with Chloe, who was standing next to him. "How many of you anticipate that you will sing at the same time as dancing onstage in the future?"

Pop put up her hand, and Chloe and Marmalade did the same. Several others in the class did as well.

"Right," said Mr. Penardos. "Gather round,

everyone. You'll all get a chance to try this, but for now we'll mic up Marmalade and see how he gets on. With a radio microphone like this you have to wear a power pack, as well as the headset."

Mr. Penardos helped Marmalade to fix the tiny microphone so that it sat comfortably. It felt strange to Marmalade, at first, to be wearing the slim headset in his long, curly hair. The small power pack was less of a nuisance, and fitted perfectly on the waistband of his trousers.

"Now," said Mr. Penardos, when Marmalade was fixed up. "The sound is transmitted to a pickup, which amplifies it through a small speaker like the one I have here. Onstage, of course, the sound is fed into the mixing desk and the sound engineer makes sure it comes out at the right level."

"How does it feel?" Chloe asked Marmalade, her eyes shining with excitement.

"Great!" said Marmalade. "It makes me feel very professional."

"Okay!" said Mr. Penardos, clapping his hands.

"We'll go through the routine now. Marmalade, you can sing along. I will turn our music down a bit so we can hear you. See how you manage with singing and dancing at the same time. I know that a lot of artists mime while they dance, but if you can manage both it's so much better."

They set off, and Marmalade's voice came out of the little speaker. Of course, Marmalade and his friends had often sung along for fun when they danced, but this was different. The pressure was on, because Marmalade knew everyone was listening to his voice. He had to concentrate hard on his breathing, because his dancing threatened to make his singing sound breathless.

When he finished his routine, everyone clapped. "Well done," said Mr. Penardos. "You did ver' well. And practice will make you even better. Singing and dancing together is quite a knack, but it is an important skill for any performer to master."

"He looked terribly serious while he was dancing," said Pop. "I've never *seen* Marmalade look so serious before!"

"That's what concentration does," Mr. Penardos said with a smile. "Bu' you're right, Pop. Marmalade was singing and dancing a happy song with a serious face. Expression is something else that you have to get right. And you need to be able to express the emotion of the song not just through your voice and facial expression, but also your whole body."

"It's an awful lot to get right at the same time," said Chloe.

"Of course it is," Mr. Penardos agreed. "And it's important not to overdo it, bu' people do hold their bodies in different ways when they feel different emotions. Let's see how each of you would move if you were feeling sad. Then you can try all the different emotions you can think of."

When Marmalade started to express happiness, he went into a pirouette as he so often did when he was full of beans. But this time he wasn't concentrating, and he fell over. Everyone laughed.

"You've forgotten about spotting during your pirouette," Mr. Penardos told Marmalade as he got up,

grinning ruefully. "You of all people should be able to do
that. Don't forget that your head should be the last part
of you to turn and the first to arrive, and keep those
eyes focused on a spot at eye level or you'll fall again.
Jack, can you pirouette?"

"Yes," said Jack quietly.

"Go on, then," Mr. Penardos said. "Do a few and
show Marmalade how it's done."

Marmalade had to stand by and watch while Jack
executed a series of perfectly balanced turns. Jack's
ballet training had given him great poise. He made the
pirouettes look effortless.

Chloe was very impressed. "That's fantastic," she
enthused when Jack had finished. "And they look really
serious somehow. When Marmalade does them,
they're just a laugh."

"It's all to do with *emotion*," Marmalade told her
quickly.

Mr. Penardos laughed. "Yes, it is," he agreed, "and
Marmalade is very good at being funny when he
dances. But don't do any more careless moves," he

added to Marmalade. "I've seen you fooling around in the corridor. You don't want to get an injury, do you?"

Marmalade shook his head, hating to be told off in front of Jack.

"Okay," said Mr. Penardos. "There's just time to shower before your next lesson. Off you go." He picked up the discarded headset and turned away.

Danny caught up with Marmalade at the showers. "He was right about you dancing around between lessons," he told Marmalade. "Don't risk your Rising Stars place, will you? It's not worth it."

"It would be terrible to get injured," agreed Jack seriously.

But Marmalade was in no mood to listen to either of them. For a start, he hadn't liked being upstaged by Jack. He didn't usually mind falling, and normally made a joke of it, but with Jack on hand to show how a pirouette *should* be done, Marmalade felt as if he'd been made to look silly. He also resented Danny warning him about the Rising Stars Concert.

"I know *exactly* what I'm doing," he told them both.

"I *need* to practise all the time. And you use your drumsticks all over the place," he added to Danny. "I've seen you! On the walls, on your knees, on tables…but no one tells you not to use them without your drum kit!"

Danny opened his mouth and then closed it again without speaking. Marmalade could tell that he wasn't persuaded by the comparison of dancer and drummer. After all, no one could argue that Danny's drumming on the walls was dangerous. But Marmalade wasn't about to stop leaping and twirling all day long. It was just the way he was. He'd been born with springs in his feet and he didn't want to just walk sensibly from place to place. Why *should* he stop? Dancing was his whole life. He couldn't bear to keep it strictly to dance studios and performances. Anywhere would do for him. And nothing anyone said would make him change his mind!

6 Turning Over a New Leaf

Whatever Marmalade felt about dancing, clowning around during lessons had to stop for a while. Mrs. Pinto and the other teachers were insisting that he concentrated on catching up with his academic work, and he couldn't ignore them any longer. It wasn't easy being sensible, and it would have been much more fun to carry on being the class joker, but Marmalade knew that if he didn't make more of an effort he would end up having to go and see the Principal. Mrs. Sharkey could be seriously scary, and Marmalade didn't want to risk being told off by her!

So he tried harder in class, and also started to work seriously on his dance assignment for Mr. Penardos.

Lucky Break

He had chosen a great piece of jazz for his dance, and had decided to portray each instrument as it was highlighted in the piece. Already he knew that one of his favourite parts was going to be the piano. As the music played, he was going to portray himself running down the keyboard and picking out individual notes. There was lots to think about while he planned his steps, and Marmalade was also helping Jack out with his dance, giving him the benefit of all his knowledge, although Jack was asking him fewer and fewer questions as he got used to the school and became more proficient at modern dance.

Marmalade was making so much effort that he felt as if he might burst, so between lessons he had to let off steam. He began to behave even more outrageously than before. Remembering what he'd read about street dancers using cardboard to cut down friction on unsuitable surfaces, Marmalade begged an old cardboard box from the kitchen and during breaks could be found almost anywhere, perfecting his spins on his shoulders, back and even his head!

Several other people had a go, but no one could beat Marmalade at his new hobby. And he didn't neglect his jumps either. He wanted to incorporate street dancing and ballet into his freestyle dance, so he was constantly startling the other students by leaping and bounding all over the place. He wanted his routine to be really original, and he planned on including some difficult jumps that would take a lot of practice to get right. Maybe, if his routine was good enough, he really would soon be dancing on television!

One day, Chloe met him rushing along the corridor on the way to a very late lunch after spending too long practising backflips on the front lawn. "I'll come and talk to you while you eat," she told him. "Everyone else has finished and gone outside to enjoy the sun."

"I was watching Jack dance this morning," Chloe told him as he joined her at a table with a large salad and a glass of milk. "He was practising in the small dance studio and I watched through the window. He's very good, isn't he?"

"He's all right, I suppose." Marmalade wasn't sure

he liked Jack being praised. He was too used to being top dog himself. "Jack needs to get more power in his movements," he told Chloe. "I keep telling him to try weight training, but he won't. How can I help him if he won't do what I say?"

Chloe laughed. "I think he's been very patient, listening to you so much," she told him. "How's your dance coming on?"

"Brilliant! It's great fun," said Marmalade. "But I want it to be really original, so Mr. Penardos can see how much effort I'm putting into it."

"Well, I think you've got some competition from Jack," said Chloe. "His dance is different from anything I've seen at Rockley Park. It's so graceful, like a mixture of ballet and modern dance."

Marmalade shook his head. "It's no good being *too* much like ballet," he told her, feeling more and more annoyed that she was so impressed with Jack's dance.

"Why not?" she asked.

Marmalade scrambled for an answer. "Because... because he might get teased," he said.

"Don't be silly!" Chloe laughed. "His dancing was brilliant. It doesn't matter what the style is, no one here will laugh at a good performance." She looked at his grumpy face. "You're not jealous, are you?" she asked.

"Of course not!" said Marmalade. "Whatever gave you that idea?"

"Don't worry," Chloe said. "He hasn't been here long enough to be chosen for the Rising Stars Concert *this* time. Anyway, I've got to go. See you later."

Marmalade stared at Chloe's back as she wound her way between the tables and out of the dining room. Jack? The Rising Stars Concert? What was Chloe on about? Marmalade had been giving Jack lots of advice, but he hadn't been paying attention to what the other dancer was really capable of. Mr. Penardos had told Marmalade that Jack was very talented, but Marmalade had conveniently forgotten this, while handing out advice and telling Jack what to do all the time.

I must pay more attention to what he's up to, Marmalade told himself as he finished his lunch. He felt embarrassed now that he'd been so keen to offer Jack advice, and hadn't bothered to pick up many tips himself. There must be loads more than the odd ballet term that Jack could help Marmalade with if he actually asked.

But Marmalade knew he couldn't bring himself to ask much advice from Jack. It wouldn't do for the best dancer in the class to get help from the new boy. He would just have to watch what Jack was doing and learn from him that way.

And if Chloe was *that* impressed, Marmalade would have to make sure his dance was something *really* special or he might lose his reputation for being the best dancer. That would *never* do!

After all, he told himself as he made his way to his next lesson, *I know I'm the best, and I must make sure I stay the best!*

7 Picking Up Tips

After tea, Marmalade watched Jack rehearsing. Chloe had been right. He was dancing well, and very differently from anyone else. Marmalade wasn't really jealous. It wasn't in his nature to feel envious of other people's lives. He would rather make the most of his own. But he *was* worried. Marmalade could see that while Jack had been soaking up information like a sponge, he himself had been too complacent. To keep ahead, he needed to pick up some tips of his own.

Now he was properly taking notice of Jack's skills, Marmalade could see that Jack had been politely listening to all his advice, but sensibly only using the bits of it that were useful to him. Marmalade would have blushed, if he were the sort of person who blushed easily!

Instead of feeling embarrassed, Marmalade thought carefully. Perhaps he could learn from Jack without seeming to... Big jumps were Marmalade's favourite part of dancing and he wanted to put a couple of really spectacular ones into his routine. Jack wasn't really into big jumps, but he knew all the theory, so all Marmalade had to do was pick his brains. Mr. Penardos was sure to be impressed if Marmalade could come up with some totally accurate classic leaps in his jazz routine. The music he'd chosen would be perfect. Marmalade could just see himself flying from his piano dance into his portrayal of the double bass and again into the saxophone solo.

But the evening was moving on and it would soon be homework time. Marmalade would have to wait until the next day to put his plan into action.

"Hey, Jack! Can I have a word?" he asked straight after breakfast the next morning, as everyone was gathering their belongings for the first lesson of the day. It wasn't the best time to ask about dancing, because they had a maths lesson to get to, but Marmalade couldn't wait any longer to start working on his idea.

"Sure!" agreed Jack.

"You know that jump I did some time ago, and you told me its proper name?"

"Yes?" replied Jack, looking puzzled.

"I can't remember what you're supposed to do with your legs," Marmalade told him.

"It doesn't matter," Jack replied. "Your jump was great."

"Yes, I know that," agreed Marmalade casually. "But I can't remember what you said, and it's been annoying me."

Jack picked up his bag and shrugged it over his shoulder. He looked pleased to be asked about his specialist knowledge. "I'm not that good at jumps," he said, "but I know how it's supposed to go. I'll show you at lunchtime, if you like. We could try it in the small dance studio before afternoon lessons."

"You don't need to *show* me," said Marmalade. "Just tell me and I'll do it now. You can say if I've got it right or not. I've been thinking about that jump all night and I want to get it sorted out."

Jack sighed. "You're supposed to have one foot pulled up to the other knee for a classic *saut de basque*," he told him. "But you're not going to do it in here, are you?"

"Of course," said Marmalade, pushing a table to one side to make room.

"But..."

It was too late. Marmalade had already taken off. Several people turned to watch. Marmalade was always fun to see when he was fooling about. Several people whistled as he landed perfectly. Marmalade turned to Jack in triumph. "How was that?"

Jack nodded. "Not bad," he admitted.

"But not perfect?" Marmalade insisted.

"Well, your foot could have been a little closer to your knee," Jack admitted. "But don't do another one here, Marmalade." He moved to get in Marmalade's way to prevent him jumping, but Marmalade pushed him away.

"Right!" Marmalade took a deep breath and leaped again. This time, the jump was perfect and beautifully executed. He threw Jack an excited, triumphant glance, but as his leading foot hit the floor it slid disastrously away from him. He could do nothing to recover his balance, and he landed heavily, amongst bags and people's feet, ending up half underneath a table.

For a moment, there was a shocked silence, and then everyone began to laugh.

"Typical Marmalade!" said Pop with a giggle.

"What a joker," agreed Ed.

"What a show off!" Tara added, folding her arms and looking down her nose at the fallen dancer.

"Are you all right?" asked Chloe between giggles. "Do you want a hand?"

"I'll pull you out," Danny offered, reaching out a hand to help his friend.

"No!" cried Marmalade, his voice high with fear. "Don't touch me!"

"What's the matter?" asked Chloe.

Marmalade stared wildly at Danny. His frightened face was deathly white and full of pain, and his leg was twisted awkwardly underneath him.

"He's hurt!" said Jack. "Don't move him. If you do, it could make things worse."

"Get Sister O'Flannery!" Danny yelled. "Tell her Marmalade has injured his leg! Go on, Chloe. Hurry!"

Chloe raced off and Lolly went with her. Danny made everyone else move back to give Marmalade some space. Very carefully, he and Ben pulled the table away from the fallen dancer. Marmalade felt so small and helpless, lying there on the dining-room floor while everyone else stood around, staring at him with worried expressions on their faces. He didn't dare to move in case he injured his leg even more and it was so painful he was sure he wouldn't be able to stand on it. Why hadn't Jack saved his explanations until they were somewhere else? It was all his fault that Marmalade was injured!

Danny crouched beside Marmalade to keep him company. "I'm sure Sister won't be long," he told him. "Don't worry. Just stay still."

But Marmalade's face was twisted in agony. "I'm scared," he whispered to Danny. "I'm afraid I might have hurt myself badly. What if it's really serious?"

8 Bad News for Marmalade

Sister O'Flannery was in charge of sickbay. It wasn't long before she arrived in the dining room, and was kneeling at Marmalade's side. She asked him exactly what had happened.

"I expect it's just a bad sprain," she told him after he had explained how he fell. "But you ought to have an X-ray to make sure. You haven't hurt yourself anywhere else, have you?"

Marmalade shook his head.

"Good," said Sister. "Don't worry. I'm going to call an ambulance. We don't want to risk making matters worse by taking you to hospital ourselves. Just keep that leg as still as you can until they come."

"Will I be able to dance again soon?" Marmalade asked anxiously.

"Goodness, I hope so!" she told him with a smile. "Let's have some space here," she added, raising her voice to address the other students. "Come on, there's nothing to see. Off you go to your lessons. Do you want someone to stay with you?" she added quietly to Marmalade.

He nodded.

"What's your name?" she asked Jack, who was standing anxiously behind Marmalade. "Can you stay with your friend?"

"Of course," Jack replied.

Marmalade shook his head violently. "No!" he cried. "I don't want Jack to stay. It was his fault I got injured! Where's Danny?"

Jack's face went almost as pale as Marmalade's. He hesitated for a moment, and then turned and left the room.

It wasn't too long before the ambulance arrived. The paramedics lifted Marmalade carefully onto a stretcher and carried him to the ambulance.

"You'd better go to your lesson now," Sister told Danny, once Marmalade was safely in the ambulance. "I'll go with him. And don't you worry – he's in good hands. We'll soon get him sorted out."

In the casualty department, it seemed ages before Marmalade could be seen, but eventually a friendly doctor took a look at his injured leg. Marmalade tried not to cry out when she moved it gently, but it really hurt, and his knee was becoming very swollen.

"We'll take an X-ray, but I think you've torn a ligament in your knee," the doctor told him. "Did you say you were a dancer?" she added.

"Yes," said Marmalade anxiously. "Will I be able to dance again soon? There's a really important concert in a few weeks' time and I need to practise for it."

The doctor shook her head. "I'm sorry," she said. "You'll have to forget about performing for the time being. Ligaments can take a long time to heal," she told Marmalade. "If you want to stand the best chance of it mending properly, you'll need to keep the weight off your leg for quite a while. Then you'll need physiotherapy to get your muscles working properly again. If you want to be a professional dancer, you'll need to give this injury every chance to mend completely. You don't want to risk it happening again and threatening your career."

"*Could* it happen again?" asked Marmalade, holding back his tears. How could he dance for the Rising Stars Concert if he couldn't practise?

"There will always be a weakness where there has been an injury," the doctor told him. "But you're young, and with any luck you won't get any problems in the future. It might be best to put your leg in plaster for a while, but we'll have a look at the X-ray before we make a decision."

Marmalade was appalled. He had been worrying about the Rising Stars Concert, but it might be that he'd *always* have a weakness in his knee because of one crazy jump. How could he have been so stupid as to jeopardize his career in this way?

Marmalade was taken to the X-ray department in a

wheelchair, and afterwards he had to wait until the doctor made a final decision.

"Well, the good news is that there are no broken bones," the doctor told him cheerfully. "I'm confident that it's the ligament at the side of your knee that's causing the trouble." She looked at Marmalade sternly. "I'm going to give you some crutches, and put a really strong elasticated bandage on your knee. You must promise me not to put any weight on your leg for at least the next two weeks."

Marmalade nodded. He'd do absolutely *anything* to help his knee heal properly.

"All right, then," she said. "We'll do that. You'll need to keep the leg up as much as possible, and no doubt Sister O'Flannery will keep a close eye on you."

She turned to the school nurse. "Make an appointment to get his knee reassessed in a couple of weeks' time," she told her. "If you're worried in the meantime, do take him to his doctor. The main thing is to try and prevent a weakness by letting the ligament heal as well as possible. You can put a cold compress on his knee to help the swelling go down. Frozen peas are good for that – wrapped in a towel, not put straight onto his skin. But I'm sure you know that already."

Sister nodded. "I keep a couple of ice packs handy in case of sprains," she said. "But I thought this looked a bit more serious."

"You did the right thing," agreed the doctor. "It's a nasty injury, but hopefully it'll mend well." Then she looked at Marmalade. "Whatever you do, don't twist your knee while it's healing," she warned him. "That will just make things worse. Don't worry too much, though," she added. "I expect you'll be dancing again next term if you take it steady."

Marmalade tried to smile and thank her, but his mouth twisted the wrong way, and he almost burst into tears. How could he bear it if he couldn't dance for the next three months? This had to be the worst moment of his entire life.

Back at school, Sister helped Marmalade into sickbay. "You'll be better sleeping here for at least the first few days," she told him. "Getting upstairs to your

own room will be difficult with crutches, and here all
your friends will be able to visit you while you keep that
leg up." She looked at him with concern. "I was going
to suggest that you went to classes this afternoon," she
said, "but you look worn out. Why don't you make a list
of things that you'd like bringing from your room? I'll get
you a glass of water so you can take those painkillers
the hospital gave us and then you can rest for a bit.
Meanwhile, I'll let your family know what's happened."

She gave him a piece of paper and a pencil, and
Marmalade tried to think of everything he'd need. By
the time he'd finished his list, the painkillers were
beginning to work. With the pain easing to a dull ache,
he eventually drifted off into an uneasy sleep.

He woke much later to find Sister putting a cup of
tea and a couple of biscuits by his bed. "You've got a
visitor!" she told him cheerfully.

It was Danny. He'd brought spare clothes,
Marmalade's wash bag, his school bag and the book
he was reading. Marmalade struggled to sit up. His
knee throbbed, and the thick bandage prevented him

from moving it easily. "What time is it?" he asked Danny groggily.

"Teatime!" Danny told him. "I came to see you after lunch, but Sister said you'd only been back from hospital a little while and had gone to sleep."

Marmalade ate a biscuit and suddenly felt ravenously hungry, realizing that he'd missed lunch. He gobbled the other biscuit down quickly as Sister came back in with a large tray. "Do you want this salad?" she asked. "I kept it in the fridge for you."

"Thanks!" he said.

"We made you this," Danny announced, putting a huge card on Marmalade's bed. "Well, Pop did the making and then we all signed it."

"Thanks, Danny! Please thank them all very much." Marmalade looked at the beautifully cut-out paper flowers that were stuck onto the front of the card. Inside, everyone had written little messages and signed them. Most of them were variations of *Get well soon,* but Jack had written *I'm so sorry* next to his name.

Lucky Break

Marmalade put the card to one side. Somehow, it was spoiled by having Jack's name on it. He didn't want to think about Jack, but he couldn't help it. If Jack hadn't come to Rockley Park, Marmalade wouldn't have asked about the jump and none of this would have happened. Everything was Jack's fault.

Somewhere at the back of Marmalade's mind, he knew he wasn't being fair, but in all his pain and misery, he couldn't bear to accept any of the blame for injuring himself. What was more, thinking about Jack was reminding him that Jack could still dance, and he couldn't. How would he cope if he could never dance again?

9 A Friend in Need

It wasn't long before Marmalade had mastered his crutches and was back at lessons again. Everyone was very kind to him, and Danny was a great help, making sure no one got too close and knocked his knee. Marmalade tried to stay cheerful, but he couldn't help thinking that there wasn't much to be cheerful about. It seemed that the class comedian had gone for ever.

After he had moped at the side of the dance studio for a couple of lessons, Mr. Penardos had a word with him. "You might as well skip my lessons until your leg is better," he said. "I had thought you might be interested in watching, but that's obviously too frustrating for you."

"Sorry," Marmalade apologized.

"Tha's all right," Mr. Penardos said. "I un'erstand how you feel. But use your time wisely. Make sure you catch up on all that academic work instead."

Marmalade did try to concentrate on his schoolwork, but every time he went somewhere quiet to study, his mind wandered to that awful moment when his foot had slid from under him and he'd realized he was in trouble. It had been landing in a slippery puddle of spilled drink that had made him fall, not a badly executed jump, but knowing that didn't help. Time after time, he replayed the jump and the painful consequences in his head. He knew he shouldn't have been dancing in the dining room, but because he was distraught that he couldn't dance, and because he couldn't bear to think it was his own fault, Marmalade continued to blame Jack.

His friends did their best to help, but nothing could make Marmalade happy. Talking to his family on the phone made him feel even more sorry for himself. He missed them badly now that he wasn't enjoying himself dancing. Their cards and presents made him feel even more homesick, so after a few days he got permission to go home for a weekend.

Marmalade's dad arrived to pick him up, and Danny carried his bag out to the car while Marmalade followed on his crutches.

Jack was loitering by the front door. He looked as if he wanted to say something.

"Have a good time," said Danny. Marmalade frowned and glanced in Jack's direction. How could he have a good time when he was injured? Jack blushed and disappeared indoors, looking upset.

At home, everyone wanted to look after Marmalade. His mum made him lie on the sofa and even his sisters tried to make him feel better. They took it in turns to bring him drinks and ran to open doors for him. They even let him watch his choice of TV programmes! His knee gradually began to feel a little better and by the end of the weekend it wasn't quite as painful.

By the time he got back to school, Marmalade was able to get up the stairs to his own bedroom. From then on things were as back to normal as they could be for a dancer who couldn't dance. Sister was very pleased with the way he was looking after his injury.

"Carry on being patient and I'm sure it will heal really well," she encouraged him. "It just needs time."

But Marmalade was getting more and more gloomy. He had lots of time to devote to all the work he liked least, while the lessons he loved most of all were denied him. He was sinking into a deep depression, and nothing his friends did could bring him out of it. Lots of students were practising hard in the hope of being picked for the Rising Stars Concert, and this made Marmalade feel even worse. He had been so sure he was going to be chosen as a Rising Star this term, but now all his dreams had turned to disaster. Everyone around him was focused and busy, while Marmalade was totally miserable. But he hadn't reckoned on his best friend.

Danny had been trying hard to keep Marmalade cheerful, but it almost seemed that Marmalade didn't *want* to be happy any more. Things came to a head when Danny came into their room to get changed after the general dance lesson. Marmalade was lying on his bed, reading a book. He didn't even look up when Danny greeted him.

Danny came over to Marmalade's bed and took the book out of his hand.

"Hey!" Marmalade protested. "That's not fair! I can't fight you for it because of my knee."

"You spend too much time thinking about your knee," Danny told him, putting the book well out of Marmalade's reach.

"Don't be so mean," said Marmalade sulkily. "I thought you were my friend."

"I *am* your friend," Danny told him. "And I'm worried about you. You spend all the time thinking about yourself, and it's not doing you any good."

"*You'd* be totally miserable if you couldn't play the drums for months," argued Marmalade.

"I know," agreed Danny. "Of course I would. But you have to get on with life, even when things go wrong."

"I can't get on with life," Marmalade told him. "My life is over."

"That's just not true!" Danny told him angrily. "And you're not the only one who's suffering. What about poor Jack?"

Marmalade stared at Danny. "What do you mean?" he demanded. "Jack hasn't injured himself. It was his fault I got hurt. If he hadn't come to Rockley Park, I would never have tried that jump."

Danny shook his head. "You can't blame Jack for your mistake," he said. "You've always fooled around, doing dance steps and jumps all over the place."

Marmalade didn't answer. He couldn't allow himself to admit that Danny was right.

But Danny hadn't finished. "Since you've been ignoring him, Jack has started to make friends of his own," he told Marmalade. "But he's so miserable about your injury. I've told him it wasn't his fault you got hurt, but he blames himself for explaining it in the dining room. He feels really guilty, and he doesn't know what to do. You made it clear that you didn't want him hanging around you any more, so he can't even say he's sorry. Why don't you make it up with him, Marmalade? I'm sure you'd feel better yourself if you did."

Marmalade lay back on his pillow and eased his sore knee into a more comfortable position. "But if I see him, it'll just remind me of all the dancing I can't do," he told Danny.

Danny picked up Marmalade's book and tossed it back on the bed. "You'd feel a lot better if you stopped thinking about yourself all the time," he told Marmalade again. "Make things up with Jack instead of moping around here. Go on. It's not fair on him otherwise."

Marmalade picked his book up and turned it over in his hands. "I don't know," he said slowly.

"Just talk to him," Danny said impatiently. "If nothing else, you can help *him* feel a bit better, can't you?" He waited a moment, but Marmalade didn't reply. "I'll see you later," Danny added crossly. He turned on his heel and left Marmalade alone.

For a while, Marmalade lay on his bed, deep in

thought. He didn't want to make Jack feel better. He still felt like blaming him for his own misfortune. But Danny had forced him to face up to things. And he owed Danny an apology too. He'd treated his best friend really badly this term, ignoring him while he was spending all his time with Jack, and then being really grouchy since he'd hurt his knee. Meanwhile Danny had remained a loyal friend, in spite of Marmalade's behaviour.

So Marmalade decided to try and be more positive. He swung his legs gingerly off the bed and made a grab for his crutches. He ought to go and find Jack and talk to him. It would be a start.

He made for the door and balanced on his good leg as he pulled the door open with one of his crutches. Slowly, he made his way down the corridor towards Jack's room. If he was lucky, Jack might be there, and he wouldn't have to struggle downstairs. When he reached Jack's door, Marmalade balanced again on his good leg while he reached for the handle. As he tried to grasp it, the door swung inwards. Someone was opening it from inside. Marmalade wobbled on his good leg, trying to regain his balance.

"Sorry!" said Jack as he saw Marmalade. He reached out to steady the injured dancer, but Marmalade grabbed the doorframe to save himself.

"You nearly made me fall again!" he snapped, shrugging off Jack's help.

10 An Apology

"I'm sorry," Jack apologized again. "I didn't know you were there."

"Oh." Now Marmalade was annoyed with himself. He'd set off meaning to make things up with Jack, but he'd got off to a bad start. It wasn't Jack's fault that Marmalade had gone to his door just then. He let go of the doorframe and headed carefully towards Jack's bed. He needed to sit down after the shock of almost falling again.

"Can I sit here?" he asked. Jack nodded, and Marmalade settled himself down. He lifted his leg carefully onto the bed and allowed Jack to prop the crutches against the bedside cupboard. Then

Marmalade leaned back against the headboard and sighed.

For a few seconds, there was silence and then they both started speaking at the same time.

"I'm sorry..." started Marmalade.

"What did..." began Jack.

Marmalade smiled wryly. "Look," he said to Jack. "I'm sorry. I came to apologize for shutting you out since my fall, but now I've gone and been horrible again! I can't get anything right at the moment. I think people are getting really fed up because we're both so miserable," he added. "And it's my fault."

Jack looked awkward. "Well I wanted to come and tell you how sorry I was, but you weren't speaking to me..." He glanced at Marmalade's leg and then looked away again.

"I know." Marmalade moved himself carefully into a more comfortable position. "All this," he said reluctantly, waving his hand at his knee. "It wasn't really your fault. I was being stupid. I know that now."

"But I shouldn't have gone along with it," said Jack.

"If I'd refused to explain until we were in the dance studio, it wouldn't have happened."

"Not just then, maybe," Marmalade admitted. "But sooner or later I'd probably have messed up. I didn't stop to think about the floor being wet. How daft was that? People are always spilling drinks in the dining room! And you didn't *make* me do that jump, did you?"

Jack shook his head. "Suppose not," he agreed.

"Danny said you've made a couple of friends," Marmalade continued after a moment.

Jack looked enthusiastic. "I've always got on really well with Ravi," he said. "And George as well."

"Well, that's good," said Marmalade, still feeling awkward.

Jack nodded. "So do you need anything?" he asked.

Marmalade thought for a moment. "There is *one* thing you could do for me," he said tentatively.

"What?" asked Jack.

"Could you tell me how the dance lessons are going?" Marmalade asked him. "I thought it would be better if I didn't turn up for classes, but I think it's even worse not knowing what's going on."

"Really?" asked Jack.

"Really," agreed Marmalade, grinning for the first time in ages. "Tell me what's been happening," he asked eagerly. "I want to know everything."

"Well," began Jack, his face lighting up, "yesterday in the general class, Mr. Penardos got me to demonstrate how ballet dancers walk across stage. It was really funny. To start with, no one could get it right except Pop and Lolly. You know how worried I was about other people knowing I was into ballet?" he added.

Marmalade nodded.

"Well, everyone was really interested. No one teased me at all! I had a great chat with Pop and Lolly afterwards. It turns out they did ballet classes for years when they were little."

For the next half hour, Jack kept Marmalade amused by relating all that had happened in the classes Marmalade had missed. Eventually, they got round to his freestyle dance.

Lucky Break

"How's your own dance routine?" asked Marmalade. "Have you finished it yet?"

"Sort of," Jack told him. "But I don't think it's that good. It needs a theme to make it hang together. At the moment it's only a series of different steps and it's just not that interesting."

"Show me," demanded Marmalade. "Move that mat first, though," he added as Jack went to the middle of the room. "We don't want any more accidents! This floor is pretty good, but just walk through the dance. And for goodness' sake, don't do any jumps!"

As Jack went through his routine, Marmalade realized how much he was enjoying himself. He felt happy for the first time since his accident. He might not be able to dance at the moment, but perhaps he *could* be of some use after all.

"There's nothing wrong with your movements," he told Jack. "But I can see what you mean. Each step is great, but the routine doesn't really hang together. You're right. Every dance *should* tell some sort of story, otherwise it's just an exhibition of your skill."

An Apology

"Why don't you come to the next lesson?" said Jack. "Even though you can't dance at the moment, you're good at making suggestions. You might be able to help the others, too."

"I don't know," said Marmalade. "But I suppose that if I did, at least I'd be involved." He moved slightly on the bed and a painful twinge ran through his knee. It was the first time he'd been reminded about his injury since he'd been talking about dancing. Danny had been right. He *did* feel better when he stopped thinking about himself all the time. But then he remembered that he still couldn't dance, and this year's Rising Stars Concert would be going ahead without him. What if this had been his best chance of performing? What if Jack or one of the other students was chosen instead of him next time? How could he bear it? But he mustn't think like that. He had to try and get on with things somehow.

"All right," he agreed, ignoring the pain. "I'll try. I *will* come to the next lesson."

11 A Project for Marmalade

Now Marmalade had a reason for getting back into dance classes, he was beginning to feel a lot better. But he still had to find Danny to thank him for sorting him out.

It was time for tea, so Jack and Marmalade went over to the dining room together. When he hobbled in with Jack by his side, all their friends looked up in surprise, but when they saw Marmalade's old grin back on his face, they gave a ragged cheer. Pop pulled out a chair so Marmalade could sit down and Jack hung Marmalade's bag over the back of it.

"Aren't you joining us, Jack?" asked Chloe.

He shook his head. "Thanks, but Ravi is waiting for me," he said. "I told him I'd have tea with him."

"See you later, then," said Danny as Jack made his way over to Ravi's table.

"Well," Tara said to Marmalade. "Why are you looking so pleased with yourself? I thought that silly grin had gone for good."

She sounded as grumpy as always, but Marmalade could tell that even Tara was pleased to see him looking more like his old self again.

"It's all Danny's fault," said Marmalade, grinning at his friend. "He cheered me up. Thanks, mate," he added, really meaning it. "I will try not to be such a miserable idiot from now on."

"You've had a hard time," said Lolly sympathetically. "It's no wonder you've been a bit miserable."

"A *bit* miserable?" said Tara. "He's been *terrible* since his accident."

"So what's changed your mood?" asked Chloe. "After all, you still can't...you know...dance."

"Don't remind me!" said Marmalade. "No, it's just that I've been giving Jack some tips for his dance routine, and I'm really enjoying doing it now that I don't have one of my own to concentrate on. I'm going to go to his next dance class and see if I can help some more. At least I'll be involved with dancing, even if I'm not doing it myself yet."

The very next afternoon, Marmalade was as good as his word and turned up for the dance class. And when he heard what Marmalade wanted to do, Mr. Penardos was very enthusiastic.

"This is splendid, Marmalade," he said. "If you find you enjoy choreography or teaching, you will never be out of a job. You know we teach choreography when you get further up the school? Why don' you watch what everyone has been doing and see if you have any suggestions."

Marmalade sat at the side of the room and watched as the dancers limbered up and then went through their routines. He itched to join them on the specially sprung dance floor, but he did his best to forget about himself and concentrated on watching the other students.

He came up with a few useful comments for Alice as well as Jack, and Mr. Penardos was full of praise. "Well done, Marmalade," he said. "Maybe you will be a famous choreographer one day!"

Marmalade tried to feel excited about being a choreographer, but although he enjoyed working out steps for himself, he knew that actually dancing them would always be his greatest love.

Near the end of the lesson, Marmalade suggested a sequence of steps to Jack, but when Jack tried them he couldn't get them quite right. "No," Marmalade told him, not sure if he hadn't explained properly or if it was just that Jack couldn't do the steps. He picked up his crutches and struggled to his feet. "I'll show you," he said.

"Be careful," Jack warned him anxiously.

"I'm all right," Marmalade replied. "Do it with me. I'll try to explain again. You lead with the right foot, and bring the left one over like this."

It wasn't easy on crutches, and he had to remember that he still mustn't put any weight on his bad knee, but Marmalade managed to show Jack what he meant.

"Oh! I see now," said Jack, very pleased. "You mean like this!"

He did the sequence again and Marmalade watched closely. "Almost," he agreed. "But you're still not bringing that leg over far enough." He tried to demonstrate and almost lost his balance. One crutch slipped on the floor and Jack had to grab his arm to stop him from falling.

Marmalade had frightened himself badly, and he was annoyed at himself as well. "I'm all right," he told Jack, shaking off his help. But what if he had fallen on his already injured knee? It seemed he couldn't do the simplest things without getting into trouble. While Jack hovered nearby, Marmalade lowered himself carefully onto his chair.

"Oh, go away," he snapped, and then sighed. "Sorry," he apologized at once. "I'm all right. You go on. I'll see you later."

Mr. Penardos turned the music off and waited until everyone had left before he came to speak to Marmalade.

"You did well today," he told him.

Marmalade shrugged. He was annoyed with himself for feeling miserable again, but he couldn't seem to help it.

Mr. Penardos sat down and studied his student for a moment. "You are bound to feel frustrated from time to time," he told Marmalade. "I un'erstand how you feel."

"Do you?" asked Marmalade bitterly.

"Oh, yes," insisted the teacher. "You see, I did a similar thing to you when I was young."

Mr. Penardos was lost in thought for a moment, and Marmalade waited, intrigued to hear what his teacher had to say.

"I was quite like you," Mr. Penardos began. "I had real talent, and a great joy of dancing in my native Cuba. I had such ambition too. I was going to set South America alight with my dancing, and maybe I would even be invited to New York to perform! But none of these things happened."

"Why not?" asked Marmalade.

Lucky Break

Mr. Penardos smiled sadly. "I was foolish," he explained. "I had injured my knee in practice one day. But I had a girlfriend I wanted to impress very much, and I ignored my injury. I was dancing with my girlfriend, and it was painful, but I was determined not to stop. I was showing off so much..." Mr. Penardos shrugged. "I fell again, and that was it. I had injured myself too much, and the knee was never the same again."

"I didn't know," said Marmalade. "I just thought you'd retired from dancing because you wanted to teach."

"I came to love teaching," Mr. Penardos told Marmalade. "But to begin with, I thought my life was over. Every time I tried to dance, my knee gave way, until I had to admit my career was finished. But you..." he nodded at Marmalade, "I admire you, because you are being careful, however much you want to use that knee again. I am sure you will be fine because you are letting it heal properly, unlike me."

"I'm sorry," said Marmalade. "It must have been terrible for you."

"It was," Mr. Penardos agreed. "But it was a long time ago, and I enjoy what I do now. But, you know, you can use your feelings since the accident to improve your dancing when you are better."

"Can I?" asked Marmalade in surprise. "How can I do that?"

Mr. Penardos smiled. "You have always been good at expressing fun and happiness in your dancing," he said. "But you have found dancing sad roles much harder. Is that not so?"

"Yes!" agreed Marmalade. That was certainly true.

"Well, this injury has given you feelings I bet you never had before," Mr. Penardos said. "Would you agree?"

Marmalade nodded. He had never been as miserable or as angry or as scared as he had been since his injury.

"Well, then," said Mr. Penardos, getting up and handing Marmalade his crutches. "Think about those feelings. Keep them in your head. You can express how you feel with your body even though you are on crutches. It's surprising how much emotion people can convey even while sitting down. I could see your misery just now, although you said nothing, and were sitting still."

"Oh," muttered Marmalade. "I hadn't thought of that."

"Think of your injury as an opportunity," the teacher advised. "While that ligament is healing, you can grow too."

Marmalade got up and hitched his bag onto his shoulder. "I'll do my best," he told his teacher. "I promise, I really will!"

12 Marmalade has an Idea

While the others were changing out of their dance clothes, Marmalade went for a walk. He could get along quite quickly on his crutches now, as long as the ground was fairly level, so he headed for his favourite spot by the lake. There, he sat on a bench in the early evening sun.

His thoughts were full of Mr. Penardos's story. Somehow, Marmalade had assumed that nobody could really understand how he felt, but now he knew that Mr. Penardos had suffered a similar injury with disastrous results. The teacher's story made Marmalade even more determined to let his knee heal properly before he used it again, however long it took.

Lucky Break

At his last check-up, the doctor had told him that the more he could build up his muscles, the better they would protect his damaged ligament, so Marmalade was already working carefully on all the exercises he'd been given by the physiotherapist.

Stretching his bad leg out in front of him he looked around at the view. The lake was a beautiful place to be on such a lovely evening. The surface reflected the cloudless sky, turning the water a wonderful silvery blue. Now and then, a slight breeze ruffled the water. A couple of ducks swam towards him through the ripples, waggling their tails expectantly.

"Sorry," Marmalade told them. "I don't have any food with me today."

He gazed out over the lake, while he thought hard about everything Mr. Penardos had said. Marmalade knew he'd lived a charmed life until this accident. Everything he'd wanted had happened for him, and his happy-go-lucky character had helped him to settle easily into boarding at Rockley Park with no hint of homesickness or any other problems. Of course, he'd had small ups and downs like everyone else, but he'd never really been anything other than happy. Looking back, even his worries about his wild, ginger hair hadn't been that bad.

Now, all that had changed. His injury had given him complex feelings that he'd never had before, feelings he needed to understand if he was ever going to be a truly great dancer. Marmalade felt as if he was on the verge of understanding himself better, and through that, becoming a better dancer.

And now he was involved with dance again, what about the routine he was supposed to be helping Jack with? He'd agreed that Jack needed a story to tell, to make his routine more interesting. Could Marmalade use his recent experiences to help with that? Jack's routine wasn't going to win him a place in this Rising Stars Concert. They both knew that Jack wasn't yet a good enough dancer to be a Rising Star, and he hadn't been at Rockley Park long enough to have earned any Rising Stars points either. But with Marmalade's help, he could still show off the huge talent he had. They ought to make Jack's dance the best they could, even though no one would see it except for the rest of the class.

Then another idea flashed into Marmalade's head. If they worked hard and came up with a polished performance, maybe Jack could dance it at a school assembly? Quite often, someone would finish the Principal's assembly with a song or a piece of music. So why not a few minutes of dance? If Mr. Penardos thought it was interesting enough, Marmalade was sure he'd put it forward for consideration.

There were two more Principal's assemblies before the end of term. If he could come up with a really good theme for Jack's dance, maybe they would be in with a chance of Jack performing for the whole school. Marmalade pulled his crutches towards him and got up. He was too excited to sit still any longer. A germ of an idea had occurred to him. It would take a lot of work, and there wasn't much time, but Marmalade was sure they could do it.

He headed back to the main house as quickly as he could. With luck, everyone would be having tea by now. The gravel crunched under his crutches as Marmalade swung along, eager to find Jack and tell him about his plan. He negotiated the couple of steps up into the main hall, and made his way down the corridor to the dining room. Just then, Jack and Ravi came out and headed off towards their house. They must have finished tea already. Marmalade leaned heavily on his crutches to get his breath back.

"Jack!" he yelled. "Wait!"

The two boys stopped, turned round and waited while Marmalade hurried towards them.

"What's up?" asked Jack when Marmalade joined them.

"Nothing's the matter," Marmalade told him with a grin. "I've just had a brilliant idea for your dance routine. I think you'll like it, and if you do, I reckon it could be more than simply an exercise for you to dance in class."

"Could it?" Jack said. "How? What's your idea?"

Marmalade tapped his nose. "For your ears only," he said mysteriously. "I'll tell you after I've had my tea."

13 A Dance for Jack

It was two weeks before the end of term, and the whole school was gathered in the theatre for the Principal's assembly. The oldest students had already taken their final exams and would be leaving today. Some were hoping to go on to music college or university, while others had already got jobs lined up in the music industry.

Younger students like Marmalade and Danny, sitting together near the front, were already looking forward to the long summer holiday as a time to relax for a while. But before that, there were still two weeks of school to get through. Each student chosen to perform at the Rising Stars Concert would need every day of those two weeks to prepare. Everyone was in a fever to know who the students were going to be and today was the day they'd find out!

First, everyone had to sit through lots of tedious but important notices. At last Mrs. Sharkey, the Principal, came to the most eagerly awaited moment of the assembly.

"And so to the Rising Stars Concert," said Mrs. Sharkey, knowing full well how impatient everyone was to know who had been chosen. "The staff have looked carefully at everyone's progress throughout the year, during class work as well as performances at the school concerts. We try to have as wide a range of acts and ages as possible, but because the concert is only a half-hour programme, the numbers are very restricted. This means that the majority of students chosen are bound to be seniors." She paused, and every single student waited, breathless with excitement and anticipation. Then she started reading out the names of those chosen, and at each announcement knots of students here and there clapped their friends. After reading out five or six names, Mrs. Sharkey paused.

"We also have a few outstanding younger students," she said. "And some of them have also earned themselves places in the concert. Rosie Masters will play her latest piece on piano." Her friends cheered, and Rosie beamed all over her face. "George Guinness will play guitar." A roar went up from another part of the theatre. "Danny James has been chosen to play drums and Chloe Tompkins will sing."

Everyone near Danny and Chloe erupted in excitement. Marmalade fixed his face into the best grin he could manage and thumped his best friend on the back. "Well done!" he told him. "I knew you could do it!" The rest of their friends were congratulating Danny and Chloe, and Marmalade took his chance to turn away and hide the misery in his eyes. He didn't want to spoil their pleasure, but it was very hard to bear after Marmalade had felt so close to being chosen himself.

Chloe was sitting on the other side of Danny. She leaned over and they gave each other a big hug. "Well done!" she said. "It's amazing. We're actually going to be on television!"

"You're not wearing your black beanie any more," Danny said, trying to disentangle himself from her.

She giggled and clutched her head. "Well, my hair has grown a bit," she said, smoothing the wispy tendrils over her ears. "And anyway," she glanced at Marmalade, "someone wanted to borrow a beanie, so I've lent it to them."

The whole room was full of excited students congratulating each other, and Mrs. Sharkey was smiling for once as she watched them. As everyone started to calm down, Marmalade struggled to his feet.

"Are you all right?" asked Danny.

Marmalade nodded, trying to look more cheerful than he felt. "Fine. I just need to get out for a minute. My leg is stiff."

He made his way slowly along the aisle, and out through a side door. He was glad to get away from all the excitement in the theatre. But there was another reason for him to leave. Everyone was still involved with the assembly, and no one noticed him reach the stage door and go in. He and Jack had been secretly working on Marmalade's idea for a dance, and Mr. Penardos had been so impressed that he'd encouraged them to perform it today. But Marmalade had changed. The over-confident extrovert had gone and his belief in himself was low. In a few minutes, everyone was going to get a big surprise, and Marmalade hoped it would be a successful one.

Jack was waiting for him, holding a long, black coat he'd borrowed from Mr. Penardos.

"Are you ready?" asked Marmalade. Jack nodded. He held the crutches while Marmalade struggled into the coat. Marmalade took Chloe's black beanie from his pocket and crammed it over his hair. Jack had to help him push some of the ginger curls under the beanie, and then Marmalade pulled it right down. Without his trademark hair, Marmalade looked completely different.

Jack was wearing bright, floppy clothes that were far too big for him. The costume department had done him proud. His face was a white, grease-painted mask. He looked just like a circus clown. Threads of black string were attached to the ends of his sleeves and trousers.

Together, they crept quietly onto the stage. The curtain was down, and Mrs. Sharkey was still standing on the other side of it, talking to the assembled students.

Marmalade clambered up onto a raised platform at the back of the stage. The platform was often used for performances when different stage heights were needed. Danny always put his drum kit there when he was playing – otherwise he would be hidden behind the guitarists. But for now, the platform was empty, except for a single chair. Marmalade sat down on it and rested his crutches by his side. Jack handed him a small crosspiece made of wood and then sprawled in front of him on the stage. Marmalade quickly hooked up the strings on Jack's clothes and held the crosspiece in his lap. Then they waited in silence.

Mrs. Sharkey was coming to the end of her speech. "Before you go there's just one more thing," she said.

Lucky Break

"As you know we often round off these assemblies with a performance. Today we have a very new student, and another who has been with us for a year. Usually, our performances are pop- or rock-influenced, but because of injury, these students have opted to do something rather different. Here they are, Jack Cheung and Marmalade Stamp!"

The curtain rose, and Marmalade looked out over the audience. It was wonderful to be onstage, even under these circumstances. Then he glanced down at Jack. He was flopped convincingly on the floor. It didn't look as if he had any bones at all. Slowly, Marmalade lifted the crosspiece he was holding, and Jack started to come to life.

To begin with, the music was slow and careful, as Marmalade took the role of an old, lame puppeteer, teaching his puppet to move. Jack had to learn how to stand, how to move without falling over and how to sit down properly. The audience laughed at Jack's antics. But gradually, the mood changed and the music quickened. The puppet learned fast and soon got better and better. In no time, he was getting impatient with the strings that held him. The puppeteer tried to restrain him, but he was old and infirm, while the puppet was young and getting more exuberant by the moment.

Jack was playing his part brilliantly. And instead of everyone laughing at Jack's antics, now the audience was anxious for Marmalade's character. The pupil was stronger than his teacher now, and soon a real struggle was going on for ownership of the strings.

"Steady!" whispered Marmalade to Jack at one point. "You'll pull me over in a minute."

Jack grinned back at him, and eased up a bit.

Eventually, the old man was forced to release his puppet. Now Jack was free, he taunted the puppeteer. He danced out of reach, and performed jumps and spins that the old man would never be able to do.

The dance ended with Jack leaping out of reach, and dancing triumphantly offstage, while the puppeteer stood, leaning heavily on his crutches – a beaten, lonely old man. Once Jack had disappeared,

Lucky Break

Marmalade returned to his seat and sank down onto it. His misery was there for all to see as the music, and the dance, came to a poignant end.

For a few moments after the curtain fell, there was silence in the auditorium. Then everyone burst into applause. The dance had captivated everyone. Jack had been a perfect, cheeky, strong-willed puppet, and Marmalade had portrayed the sadness of the old man to perfection.

The boys came out to take their bows and everyone cheered them. Jack and Marmalade grinned at each other. It hadn't been the dance Marmalade had been hoping for at the beginning of term. The Rising Stars Concert was going to take place without him. But he was performing again, and it had gone brilliantly.

With any luck, over the summer, Marmalade's knee would finish healing, and he would be able to come back to school fit and well. This brief performance had done a lot to boost his confidence, and Marmalade could feel his old, buoyant self returning. But he would never risk injury again by behaving stupidly, and from now on, he would keep his fooling to jokes, rather than jumps.

"No more falls," he said to Jack above the cheers of the audience.

"Right!" Jack agreed.

"And next year we'll be Rising Stars," he promised.

"Do you think so?" asked Jack. They bowed again and the curtain came down in front of them, separating them from the audience.

Marmalade turned to Jack, determination shining in his eyes. "I know it," he said. "With our skills combined, we're unbeatable. We ought to have a pact for next year. Rising Stars!" He raised his hand and Jack did the same. They clapped their hands together and grinned.

"Rising Stars!" they promised each other. "Rising Stars!"

✳ ✳ So you want
to be a pop star?
✳

Turn the page to read some top tips
on how to make your dreams
✳ come true... ✳
✳

✳ Making it in the music biz ✳

Think you've got tons of talent?
Well, music maestro Judge Jim Henson,
Head of Rock at top talent academy Rockley
Park, has put together his hot tips to help
you become a superstar…

✳ Number One Rule: Be positive!
You've got to believe in yourself.

✳ Be active! Join your school choir
or form your own band.

✳ Be different! Don't be afraid to stand
out from the crowd.

✳ Be determined! Work hard and stay focused.

✳ Be creative! Try writing your own material –
it will say something unique about you.

✳ Be patient! Don't give up if things
don't happen overnight.

✳ Be ready to seize opportunities
when they come along.

Be versatile! Don't have a one-track mind – try out new things and gain as many skills as you can.

Be passionate! Don't be afraid to show some emotion in your performance.

Be sure to watch, listen and learn all the time.

Be willing to help others. You'll learn more that way.

Be smart! Don't neglect your school work.

Be cool and don't get big-headed! Everyone needs friends, so don't leave them behind.

Always stay true to yourself.

And finally, and most importantly, enjoy what you do!

Go for it! It's all up to you now...

Usborne Quicklinks

For links to exciting websites where you can find out more about becoming a pop star and even practise your singing with online karaoke, go to the Usborne Quicklinks Website at www.usborne-quicklinks.com and enter the keywords "fame school".

Internet safety

When using the Internet make sure you follow these safety guidelines:

✸ Ask an adult's permission before using the Internet.

✸ Never give out personal information, such as your name, address or telephone number.

✸ If a website asks you to type in your name or e-mail address, check with an adult first.

✸ If you receive an e-mail from someone you don't know, do not reply to it.

For more

read...

Reach for the Stars

Chloe wants to be a star...

Chloe totally loves singing and spends hours practising in her bedroom, miming into her hairbrush in front of thousands of imaginary fans. So when she gets the chance to audition for Rockley Park – the school for wannabe pop stars – Chloe's determined to make the grade. But first she has to persuade her parents that her ambition is for real. She knows it's going to be tough, but life in the music biz isn't all glitz and glamour.

Will Chloe get to live her dream?

0 7460 6117 X
£3.99

Get ready for the next singing sensation!

Chloe's made it into top talent academy Rockley
Park, her first step on the road to success as a
pop singer. She's desperate to perform in the
school's Rising Stars concert – she's heard that
talent scouts often turn up from the big record
companies – but she's got one problem...she
can't find her voice! Chloe's friends rally round
and try to help get the power back in her voice,
but time is running out.

Will Chloe miss her Big Chance?

0 7460 6118 8
£3.99

Secret Ambition

Lights, camera, action!

A TV crew is coming to Rockley Park school and model twins Pop 'n' Lolly are the star attraction. The talented twosome are used to doing everything together and they make the perfect double act. So Pop can't understand why Lolly seems so fed up.

Will Pop discover Lolly's secret before she ruins their glittering career?

0 7460 6120 X
£3.99

Rivals!

The competition is hot!

Danny's a truly talented drummer and he's in constant demand at Rockley Park school for the stars. But Charlie, the other drummer in his year, is jealous of Danny's success. Tension mounts between the two rivals so when they're forced to play together in the school concert sparks could fly!

They've got everything to play for, but who will come out on top?

0 7460 6119 6
£3.99

Tara really rocks!

Tara is following her dream of becoming a rock star. But when she hears about an African school for orphans she decides that raising money is more important than her ambitions. A charity CD seems like a great idea as she's surrounded by talented friends and famous teachers at Rockley Park, school for the stars.

Will Tara succeed or will she get herself into more trouble than she bargained for?

0 7460 6835 2
£3.99

Look out for more **fabulous**

titles coming soon!

Cindy Jefferies' varied career has included being a Venetian-mask maker and a video DJ. Cindy decided to write *Fame School* after experiencing the ups and downs of her children, who have all been involved in the music business. Her insight into the lives of wannabe pop stars and her own musical background means that Cindy knows how exciting and demanding the quest for fame and fortune can be.

Cindy lives on a farm in Gloucestershire, where the animal noises, roaring tractors and rehearsals of Stitch, her son's indie-rock band, all help her write!

To find out more about Cindy Jefferies, visit her website: www.cindyjefferies.co.uk